Hello Kitty

and friends

The Cupcake Mystery

·A HELLO KITTY ADVENTURE·

HarperCollins *Children's Books*

MEET

Hello Kitty
and friends

Hello Kitty

Mimmy

Tammy

Mama

Papa

Grandpa

Grandma

Fifi

Dear Daniel

With special thanks to
Linda Chapman and Michelle Misra

First published in Great Britain by HarperCollins Children's Books in 2014

www.harpercollins.co.uk
1 3 5 7 9 10 8 6 4 2
ISBN: 978-000-754069-3

Printed and bound in England by Clays Ltd, St Ives plc.

MIX
Paper from
responsible sources
FSC™ C007454

FSC™ is a non-profit international organisation established to promote
the responsible management of the world's forests. Products carrying the
FSC label are independently certified to assure consumers that they come
from forests that are managed to meet the social, economic and
ecological needs of present and future generations,
and other controlled sources.

Find out more about HarperCollins and the environment at
www.harpercollins.co.uk/green

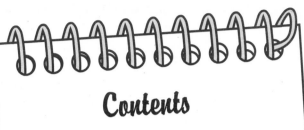

Contents

A Mystery!

Hello Kitty huffed on the window and rubbed it clear to look outside. She took a look at all the beautiful orange and yellow leaves on the trees and breathed in happily. She loved the autumn! Her twin sister, Mimmy, was sitting

Hello Kitty and friends

next to her, stringing beads for a necklace and

listening to the birds *twittering* in the trees.

For once, they had no friends round to play. It

was just the two of them on a clear and crisp

Saturday afternoon.

Suddenly someone tickled Hello Kitty's shoulder. She squealed and turned round. Papa was grinning down at her with a bag of recycling in one hand. It seemed like he was the only one doing any work that day!

Hello Kitty and Mimmy both offered to help him but he said he was only teasing. He was **enjoying** sorting out the house, tidying up all the old papers and magazines and the clothes that they had grown out of. He was going to put all the bags in the shed for now.

He went out the door and down the

garden path. Mimmy showed Hello Kitty

the necklace she had finished. It was

long enough to wear now, and

it was **beautiful!**

She smiled as she said that

Hello Kitty could have it, and she would make

another for herself. Hello Kitty grinned back as

Mimmy fastened it around Hello Kitty's neck…

CRASH!

They both jumped and looked round as they

heard the sound of breaking glass from

the shed.

Papa came through the door looking fed up. **Oh dear**. He'd been moving some things around and accidentally broken the shed window. He told the girls not to go near the shed while he cleared up the glass.

Poor Papa!

Hello Kitty helped Mimmy make another necklace for herself. Now what should they do? Mimmy said she felt like baking, and that

gave Hello Kitty a super idea. In the morning
they were going with their friend, Dear Daniel,
to visit his granny. She was feeling a bit sad
because her old dog had been re-homed a few
weeks ago. She had been finding it hard to look
after him as she couldn't walk him
every day any more. So they had
decided to go and see if they
could cheer her up.
Why didn't they make
some lovely cakes
for her?

Mimmy thought
it was definitely

a **super** idea!

They ran into the kitchen. Mama was there tidying things away, as she had been making some cupcakes of her own. They each had one of them with a big glass of milk, and then they took one out to poor Papa who was still tidying up the glass in the garden. *Yummy!* When they went back inside, Mama mentioned that the house was looking very tidy indeed now Papa had cleared away all the papers and magazines that

Hello Kitty *and friends*

had been lying around.

When they asked her, Mama smiled and said that of course the girls could do some baking, and she would help them. They got out all the ingredients they needed to make their cupcakes...

They set to work measuring and mixing. It was great fun and of course the best bit was being allowed to scrape the mixing bowl clean with their fingers!

While the cakes cooked, Mama made the girls a lovely autumn picnic to take out into the garden. She said she would take the cakes out of the oven when they were ready and then the girls could

decorate them once they were cool enough.

Hello Kitty and Mimmy wrapped up warmly

and carried their food and a picnic rug out into

the garden. It was *wonderfully* sunny

outside, and the air was clear and crisp. For

their picnic, Mama had given them...

Little sausages

Boiled eggs

Warm tea in a thermos

And they each had one more of the

cupcakes she had made, to have for pudding!

They set everything out neatly in the shade of a tree near the shed. They ate some of the sausages and boiled eggs, but after all the cake mixture they had eaten, they weren't very hungry for their cupcakes just yet!

Papa offered to eat the cakes for them. They **grinned** and told him there were more in the kitchen if he wanted

them. Papa went inside and the girls decided to
have a run round to see if that would help them
feel hungry again.

They decided to play hide and seek. They
knew all the hiding places in the garden but it
was still great fun, especially with all the piles of
autumn leaves everywhere!

They decided the
swing would be
the base and
the person
hiding had to
try and get to it
before the person

seeking caught them. Soon they both had pink cheeks from running round. It did make them hungry though!

They ran over to the picnic. But **oh no!** What had happened? The thermos of tea was turned over, the rest of the sausages were missing, and *worst* of all – Mama's lovely cupcakes were gone! There were only the

empty paper cases and a few crumbs left.

Hello Kitty and Mimmy stared at the empty plates. Maybe Papa had eaten them, suggested Mimmy?

They hurried inside to where Papa and Mama were sitting at the kitchen table. Papa was very surprised to hear about the missing cupcakes. He hadn't eaten them – he promised! They all went outside to take a look and figure out what had happened.

Mama looked at the empty plates and thought that maybe a bird had flown down and helped itself?

Hello Kitty frowned. But would a bird want

sausages? And how had it taken the cupcakes,

and left the cases behind? A bird would have had to take them away too. Mama said it **HAD** to have been a bird. What else could it have been?

Hello Kitty grinned.

Maybe it was....

A GHOST!

Mimmy gave a little squeal.

Papa told them not to be so silly. Ghosts weren't real. But he and Mama did agree it was a mystery.

Mama went inside to get the girls some more cakes as Hello Kitty nudged Mimmy – this was exciting. It was their own real mystery...

THE MYSTERY OF THE DISAPPEARING CUPCAKES!

A Strange Noise

That night, Hello Kitty and Mimmy decided they would share a bedroom. They had their own rooms, but sometimes at weekends and in the holidays they liked to be together. They would sleep in Hello Kitty's room and put up a camp bed for Mimmy to sleep on.

They decorated the

cupcakes, brushed their

teeth and then had a

bath. After that they

got into their pyjamas.

Hmmm... it still wasn't

bedtime. What could they do? Ooohh! They

decided they had just enough time to paint their

nails. Hello Kitty decided on a pretty pink polish

called Rosy Days and

Mimmy decided on a

silver sparkly polish

called Starlight.

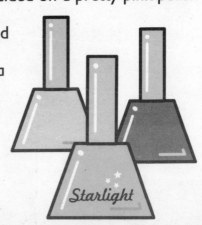

Starlight

They let their nails dry and then got into bed. But they still weren't at all sleepy so Hello Kitty decided that she would tell a bedtime story.

Mimmy hugged her teddy as Hello Kitty began.

Once upon a time there was a girl called Olivia. She lived in a big old house and there was one room upstairs that she was never allowed to go into. She sometimes went and sat outside the door and when she was there she could hear someone walking round inside…

Mimmy gave a little gasp. It wasn't a

g…g… ghost, was it?

Hello Kitty smiled. She didn't want to upset her sister. No, it wasn't a ghost. It was actually a little pixie!

Mimmy breathed out a sigh of relief. Phew! Hello Kitty went on with the story. The pixie was very sweet and friendly and could grant

wishes and when Olivia finally met him, they had

lots of adventures together!

THE END. She finished the story with a

smile. Mimmy clapped her hands and said she

was thirsty now, so they climbed out of bed and

went downstairs to get a drink.

BANG!

There was a loud noise from the kitchen and then a faint scrabbling sound. Hello Kitty and Mimmy stopped in their tracks and looked at each other. What was that?

Maybe Mama and Papa were in there? Hello Kitty listened hard.

Mimmy clutched her arm. *Maybe* it was the ghost again!

Hello Kitty reminded her that there were no such things as ghosts! She pushed open the door. The kitchen looked just like it usually did apart

from one thing. The purple vase by the window behind the sink had been knocked on to its side. The noise they heard must have been it falling over; it was still wobbling slightly.

But *how* had it fallen over? There was no one in the kitchen.

Hello Kitty *and friends*

Hello Kitty went over and put the vase back where it usually was. It must have been the wind, she whispered. The window was open. The wind must have knocked it over. That *had* to be what had happened…

Mimmy looked out of the window. There wasn't any wind. The trees were still. It was a cool autumn night without even a breeze to move the leaves.

Hello Kitty could see that her sister was thinking about ghosts again. She nudged Mimmy and told her it was probably a pixie like in the story! That made her sister smile and relax a bit.

They both got a glass of milk and went back

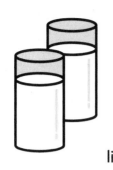

upstairs. Hello Kitty made up another

story about the pixie granting

Olivia's wish to have a pony. Mimmy

liked that story and she fell asleep with

a smile on her face just before Mama came up

to tuck them in and kiss them goodnight.

Hello Kitty *and friends*

Hello Kitty lay awake after Mama had gone. Her thoughts kept **whirling** round and round. Why had the vase fallen over in the kitchen? What had made the scrabbling noise she had heard? And did it have anything to do with the missing food that afternoon?

Hmmm. It was all **very** confusing. She couldn't wait to see Dear Daniel in the morning and tell him all about it. She decided she would also ring up their two other friends, Fifi and Tammy, and tell them about it too.

Hello Kitty, Dear Daniel, Fifi and Tammy

were such good *friends*
they had even made up
their own club – the
Friendship Club. They
liked doing things
together like baking

and making things, painting

and having trips out, and

making up rules about

friendship. They had

made a magazine,

made beauty potions,

been in a fancy dress

parade and even been on

Hello Kitty and friends

stage at a pop *concert*. But one thing they hadn't done yet was solve a... mystery!

Hello Kitty felt a tingle of excitement. Maybe it was time they became the Friendship Club Mystery Solvers!

What a Mess!

When Hello Kitty woke the next morning,

she didn't know whether to be relieved or

disappointed that nothing else strange had

happened in the night. Breakfast was very

normal. No food went missing from their plates

– sausages and eggs and bacon. **Yum!** No glasses or bowls fell over.

Mimmy seemed to have forgotten about the unusual events from the day before. She chattered happily as she helped Hello Kitty pack eight pretty cupcakes into a pink tin with a silver

heart on top. She **hoped** Dear Daniel's granny was going to like the cupcakes. It would be nice to cheer her up — she must be missing her dog a lot.

Mama drove them there. Dear Daniel was just arriving with his dad when they got to his

granny's house. Hello Kitty was longing to

tell him about the mystery but she decided to

wait until later; he was coming

back to their house after their

visit so she could tell him then.

Dear Daniel's granny was

very pleased to see them and

she L♥VED the cupcakes. She made some

cups of tea for the grown-ups

and poured some apple

juice out for Dear Daniel,

Mimmy and Hello Kitty.

She could only walk

very slowly so Hello

Kitty, Mimmy and Dear Daniel helped her carry everything and gave the drinks out.

Hello Kitty saw a photo of a dog on the mantelpiece. She went over and looked at it. Dear Daniel's granny saw her and smiled sadly – she told Hello Kitty she *really* did miss him but at least she would be able to visit him in his new home. And she just wasn't able to walk well enough now to exercise a dog.

She sighed and Hello Kitty felt very sorry. She wished there was something they could do!

They spent the morning there and then Mama dropped Mimmy at her friend Alice's house, before heading home. As Mama parked the car, Hello Kitty and Dear Daniel jumped out. Hello Kitty whispered to him that she had something exciting to tell him. Dear Daniel

wanted to know what it was straightaway but

she giggled that he would just have to wait

until they got inside! Mama opened the front

door and they ran in, but then they stopped in

surprise. They could see into the kitchen from

the hallway and there were things all over

the floor!

It hadn't been

that **messy**

when they had gone out.

They went to the doorway.

The big plate that had been on the

kitchen table with the leftover

breakfast sausages was now on the floor in

pieces and three glasses had been knocked over and were broken too! A bag of Mama's jewellery-making supplies was upside down on the floor – beads and threads were spilling out all over the place. The morning newspaper had been pushed off the sideboard and the vase by the window was knocked over again. What a *mess!*

Hello Kitty turned to Mama; what could have happened? Mama looked worried. A burglar must have broken in! She told Hello Kitty and

Dear Daniel to come outside and not touch

anything. She

would have to call

Papa and phone

the police!

Papa quickly came

home and two friendly police officers arrived;

a man and a woman. They looked through the

house but it was *very* strange – the burglar

hadn't gone into any

room apart from

the kitchen and

the only things

missing were the

46

?

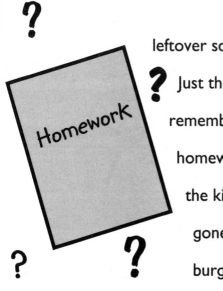

Homework

?

?

?

leftover sausages from breakfast! Just then, Hello Kitty remembered that her homework book had been on the kitchen table – and it was gone too! But why would a burglar just steal sausages and a homework book? There were even still coins on the sideboard. Nothing else had been taken at all!

The policewoman said it was very odd. The burglar must have got in through the open

? ?

?

?

?

kitchen window, although it was very *small*

so the burglar must have been small too.

Hello Kitty told the police about how she and

Mimmy had found the vase knocked over the

night before and also about how their picnic

had disappeared. The police made a note of

everything Hello Kitty said and told Mama

and Papa to be sure to let them know if

anything else happened. It was all

very strange.

When the police left, Hello Kitty and Dear

Daniel went upstairs. Now that Dear Daniel

had heard everything, he wanted to solve the

mystery too! He said they should ring Fifi and

Tammy and tell them to come round too.

Hello Kitty *and friends*

Hello Kitty knew they were both busy that day –
Tammy was decorating her bedroom and Fifi had
ice-skating practice. But Dear Daniel said they
just **HAD** to call and
tell them – they
would really
want to know.
He was
right! As soon
as Fifi and Tammy
heard what had happened
they *both* said they would change their plans
for the afternoon. They wanted to see if they
could help solve the mystery. Hello Kitty asked

Mama if they could come over and **luckily** Mama said that it was fine.

As Hello Kitty and Dear Daniel got some biscuits and juice out, Hello Kitty had a brilliant idea. Instead of this being just a Friendship Club meeting. They could rename it – a special meeting of the **Friendship Club Mystery Solvers!**

Hello Kitty *and friends*

Dear Daniel loved that idea! So, what did he and Hello Kitty need to get out?

They got out…

Notepads

Pencils

A magnifying glass

A camera for photographing clues.

There! They were all ready. Now they just needed the other Mystery Solvers to arrive!

The Mystery Solvers

Tammy and Fifi were very excited when they arrived and heard about the *Mystery Solving Club*. They all sat down in Hello Kitty's bedroom and Hello Kitty told them everything that had happened, starting with the

picnic going missing. They all agreed it was very

puzzling.

Hello Kitty and friends

Hello Kitty suggested they make some notes. **What** did they know about the thief? Everyone called things out and she wrote them all down in a list.

The thief...
- Likes sausages and cupcakes
- Likes homework books
- Is small enough to fit through the kitchen window

Hmmm. They didn't feel very close to solving the mystery! What sort of thief stole homework books? Maybe they should go and look for clues.

Dear Daniel declared they should look for strange footprints outside. The thief might have stood in some of the soft mud or soil *outside*, and they would be able to take a photograph of the footprint and show it to the police. He'd read mystery stories where clues like that had helped catch a burglar!

Fifi agreed, and put in that they should also

look more closely at the kitchen window and see if they could find any clues there. **Maybe** the thief had torn their

clothes as they had climbed in!

Hello Kitty felt a tingle of excitement run through her. This was super – maybe they really could solve the mystery on their own!

They all hurried downstairs to search the

garden for footprints first. After a minute

Tammy squealed. She had found a footprint in

one of the flower beds! They all raced over.

Hello Kitty and friends

There was a footprint in the dirt beside a rose bush. How *exciting* was that? It was really quite small though; Hello Kitty looked at her own shoes. It was only about the size of her feet. The thief must be a child!

Dear Daniel looked at the footprint, then looked at Hello Kitty's feet. He **smiled** as

he asked Hello Kitty to take off her shoe. She was surprised but did as he asked – and then he held it upside down and

showed the others that the footprint matched

the bottom of Hello Kitty's shoe perfectly! It

wasn't the thief's footprint. It was Hello Kitty's!

She must have made it **yesterday**

when she had been playing in the garden with

Mimmy.

The Mystery Solvers couldn't help giggling,

but they were very

disappointed. Still, maybe

there were some other

footprints? They

looked all around

but the **only** other

prints they found

matched Papa's boots

or Mimmy and Hello

Kitty's shoes. *Oh well*.

They decided it was time to have a look

at the window. There was nothing strange

there though – it just looked like it usually did.

They were about to turn away when Tammy's

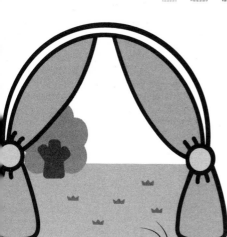

sharp eyes noticed
something.

Look!

Caught in the
wood right by the
catch were two small black hairs.
Tammy pulled them out and
they all looked at them
through the magnifying
glass. They were about
two centimetres long.
Everyone looked at each

other in excitement. *No one* in Hello Kitty's house had hair like that. Maybe this was a clue – a real clue!

Dear Daniel photographed them and Hello Kitty started a new page of her notebook with the heading CLUES. Underneath the heading she wrote…

CLUES

Two black hairs

Now the Mystery Solvers knew something else about the thief; they had black hair. But how could they find out anything more?

Ooooh!

Tammy had a fantastic idea.

They should interview Hello Kitty's neighbours and see if they had seen anything suspicious. They might have noticed someone hanging around – someone small with black hair. It might give them some more clues.

Hello Kitty *and friends*

Oh yes! Hello Kitty

liked that idea. They should

do that straight away.

They went next door and

spoke to the man who lived

there. He shook his head. He was sorry but

he hadn't seen anything suspicious. And the neighbours on the other side were away; they'd been on holiday for a whole week, so they couldn't have seen anything! *Oh dear.*

Hello Kitty *and friends*

They went back to Hello Kitty's bedroom and
sat down on the floor. What could they do now?
Everyone scratched their heads and looked
at each other. They were all out of ideas. Hello

Kitty was about to suggest they search the

garden again when suddenly...

A noise from downstairs! What on earth could

it be?

Caught!

Hello Kitty and her friends raced downstairs

as quietly as they could. They stopped in the

hall at the bottom of the staircase and *crept*

towards the kitchen with their hearts beating

fast. What if it was the burglar? Hello Kitty saw

the gap between the door and the wall and

couldn't resist having a quick peek. She held her

breath. What was she going to see?

A CAT!

There was a

black cat in the

kitchen! Hello Kitty quickly pushed the door

open and everyone huddled up to see. The cat

froze as it saw them. Turning tail, it raced

across the floor, jumped on to the window

ledge, leapt past the knocked-over vase and

escaped through the window!

They

all ran to

look outside and

were just in time to see the

cat *streak* across the lawn and

jump into the garden shed through the broken

window! Hello Kitty gasped. The cat must be

the thief! They should tell Mama and Papa

straight away!

They ran to the lounge and told Mama and Papa what they had seen. They were **very** surprised.

A cat had caused all this trouble? Mama and Papa laughed – a cat was better than a burglar any day! They all went outside to the garden shed. Papa quietly opened the door and there, nestled among the

Hello Kitty *and friends*

old clothes and newspapers, was the black cat.

And cuddled up with her were two black and

white kittens!

The kittens had big eyes, fluffy coats and

short, stubby tails.

The mother cat was skinny and looked slightly frightened.

Mama crouched down slowly and murmured encouragingly, and the black cat padded over and nuzzled her head against Mama's hand. So the thief had just been a stray cat! No wonder she had been able to get in through the small kitchen window, and the only thing she had been interested in was food. She **_must_** have been trying to feed herself and her kittens. But what about Hello Kitty's homework book, Dear Daniel pointed out. Where had that gone?

Hello Kitty *and friends*

Ah. Papa White looked rather red-faced as he spotted something and *pulled* it out from the pile of recycled papers and magazines that the cats were lying on. It was a blue homework book! Maybe he had been a bit too keen on recycling... He must have brought it out with all the rest of the old papers. Hello Kitty just hadn't

noticed it was missing until they came home and thought they had been burgled!

They all laughed, and Hello Kitty told Papa not to worry. She was just happy that the mystery had been solved!

Hello Kitty stroked the black cat, who was now **purring** loudly. She seemed very friendly. Fifi knelt down to pat her too, and wondered aloud if she had an owner.

She didn't have a collar

on but Mama suggested that if they took her

to the vet in the morning then the vet would be

able to check if she had a microchip. If she did,

they should be able to find her owner's phone

number.

But what would they do with her until then?

Oooh! Hello Kitty jumped up in

excitement. They should make the shed a

perfect little home for the mother cat and

her kittens!

And so the Friendship Club Mystery

Solvers became the Pet Carers Club

instead. They fetched the cat some milk

and water as well as some mince from the

fridge. They cuddled and stroked the kittens and played with them – they even found some old balls of string for them to pounce on and chase.

Mama thought the kittens looked about eight weeks old – just about ready to leave their mum and go to new homes.

When Mimmy came home from Alice's house she was **astonished** to see the cat and kittens there, but was soon as excited as

the others to have them to play with! She joined

in with the others, rolling the balls of string and

stroking them. They all hoped

the mother cat would have

a microchip so they

could help her get back

to her home.

Fifi declared that she

thought the Friendship

Club had done a **great**

job – they'd solved the mystery

and found the thief. Hello Kitty grinned and

agreed as she said a *big* thank you to all

her friends for dropping everything they were

doing to come and help her that afternoon.

She was so grateful — and so lucky to have such

great friends! Fifi, Tammy and Dear Daniel all

blushed and **smiled**. Tammy even thought

up a new Friendship Club rule:

Good friends are
always there, no
matter how *busy*
they are.

It was *perfect!* They all high-fived.

That was a great friendship rule and they would

always be there for each other – no matter what.

The next morning Mama, Hello Kitty and Mimmy took the little cat family to the local vet. He checked the cat and kittens over and said that apart from being a little thin they were all very healthy.

Next, the vet ran a scanner over the back of the mother's neck. There was a loud *bleep* – she did have a microchip! The vet looked up all the details from the microchip on the computer. The cat was apparently called Sooty and she belonged to a lady who lived

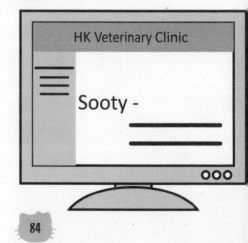

HK Veterinary Clinic

Sooty -

only a short car journey away. The vet phoned her straightaway, and **smiled** at Mama as he waved her over to speak to the lady herself. It was obvious that she was absolutely delighted that Sooty had been found. The little cat had gone missing two and a half months ago when the lady had moved into her new house.

Mama hung up and told them that the lady was going to come to their house to collect

Sooty and her kittens right away. She would take them all back to her house and then try and find good homes for the kittens. So they'd better get back quickly!

Hello Kitty thanked the vet as they left, and when she got home the **first** thing she did was phone the Friendship Club! They all came round as quickly as they could, to wait with Hello Kitty and Mimmy for the lady to arrive.

It was warm that morning so Sooty lay on the grass in the sun while the two kittens chased butterflies. They were very **cute.** One was black with four white

paws and a white chest and the other was white with a black patch on her head. They charged round after each other and then rolled in a heap together before **pouncing** on some leaves on the grass. They really were adorable! Fifi sighed; it was going to be really hard to say goodbye to them and never see them again.

Mimmy thought it was sad that they would go to **different** homes. It would be like her and Hello Kitty being separated. If only someone would give both the

kittens a home together, she put in. Everyone

nodded their heads to agree. But who would

want two kittens?

Hello Kitty frowned. **Hmmm...** An idea

started to form in her head. Leaving the others

outside, she went to find Mama and explained

her idea. Mama listened and started

to nod thoughtfully. It could

work... She would make a

quick phone call.

Hello Kitty waited

anxiously, hopping

from one leg to the other as

Mama dialled.

Through the hall window, Hello Kitty saw a car pull into their driveway. A kind-looking lady got out and hurried towards the door with a cat carrier in her hands. It **must** be the lady here to collect Sooty and her kittens!

Mama was talking on the phone now so Hello Kitty raced to open the door herself. She said hello and smiled at the lady, who she

could see was very eager to see Sooty! Hello

Kitty took her straight through to the garden.

But all the time, she kept her fingers crossed...

The lady *gasped* as she walked outside

and saw Sooty and the kittens. She called

Sooty's name, and the little black cat looked

round and gave a delighted meow. She jumped

to her feet and trotted straight over to her

owner, who knelt down to

pat her. Sooty pushed

her head against the

delighted lady's hands

and legs, purring

very loudly indeed.

Hello Kitty and her friends smiled at each other.
It was lovely to see the little cat back with her
owner, who clearly loved her very much.

The two kittens were still

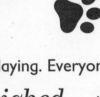

playing. Everyone looked at them, and the lady

sighed as she patted Sooty. She wished she

could keep them, but she already had two other

cats as well as Sooty. Five cats would just be

too many for her! She told the Friendship Club

that she would make sure they both went to

good homes.

Hello Kitty **smiled** and breathed that they might be able to help with that... Just as Mama White came out to the garden! She gave Hello Kitty a smile and a nod. Hello Kitty's heart leapt. Did that mean her idea had worked out?

Mama introduced herself to the lady and explained that Hello Kitty had thought of an ideal home for the kittens. There was a

Hello Kitty and friends

lovely old lady who was very lonely because she had had to have her dog re-homed. She couldn't have another dog because she wouldn't be able to walk it, but two kittens would be

perfect...

The Friendship Club all gasped. Mama must mean Dear Daniel's granny!

Mama White smiled. Yes! They were right. She'd just spoken to Dear Daniel's granny on the phone and she had said she would love to give two kittens a home.

Sooty's owner was thrilled and the Friendship Club were so happy they cheered. Now the two kittens could stay together, and the Friendship

Club could even visit them whenever they liked!

Mama fetched cups of tea for her and the

Hooray!

lady and lemonade and cookies for everyone

else, and they all sat in the garden in the sun.

Sooty curled up on her

owner's knee, purring

contentedly, and the

kittens carried on

leaping about and

playing in the grass.

Mimmy gave a

happy sigh.

Everything had worked out

after all. There wasn't a ghost

and there wasn't a burglar, and now Dear

Daniel's granny wouldn't be lonely any more!

Hello Kitty and friends

Hello Kitty grinned. Mimmy was right. It really was PURR-fect!

The end

Turn over the page for activities and
fun things that you can do with your
friends – just like Hello Kitty!

Hello Kitty's Raspberry Surprise Cupcakes!

Hello Kitty loves baking, and cupcakes are one of her favourite things to make. These ones have a surprise in the middle too – so follow the instructions and let's get baking! You'll need a grown-up helper to make these. It should make about 12 cupcakes.

You will need:

- A large mixing bowl
- A wooden spoon
- A whisk
- 2 small mixing bowls
- Scales and measuring spoons
- A 12 hole cupcake or muffin tray
- Paper cupcake cases

MAKE SURE YOU ASK MAMA OR PAPA TO HELP!

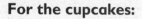

For the cupcakes:

125g of soft butter

125g of caster sugar

125g of self-raising flour

2 eggs

1 teaspoon of vanilla extract

2 tablespoons of milk

12 raspberries

For the icing:

100g of soft butter

100g of icing sugar

12 raspberries, for decorations

What to do:

1. Ask your grown-up helper to turn the oven on to 190°C (370°F / Gas Mark 5).

2. Mix the butter and sugar together in the large bowl – mix hard until they're completely combined.

3. Break the eggs into a small bowl, and whisk them until they're fluffy.

4. Tip them into the butter and sugar mixture a little at a time, stirring them as you go.

5. Add the vanilla extract and stir it through.

6. Tip the flour and the milk into the mix, and stir it until you have a nice, smooth mixture.

7. Line each hole in your cupcake or muffin tray with a paper case. Add a spoonful of cake mixture to each until it's half full.

8. Take one raspberry for each cupcake, and push it down into the middle of the mixture. Use a little more cake mix to cover it if you can still see it!

9. Ask your grown-up helper to put the tray in the oven for you, and leave it for 15–20 minutes. Your cakes should be golden on top and springy in the middle when done.

10. Ask your grown-up helper to take your cakes out of the oven and set them aside to cool.

11. Mix together the butter and icing sugar for the icing. Stir hard until it's smooth and creamy.

12. When your cakes are cool, use a butter knife or teaspoon to spread the icing on the top of each cake, and top them with a raspberry each. Delicious!

Your cakes are now ready to serve – **yummy!**

Hello Kitty Tip:

Don't forget to wash your hands before you start baking, and wear an apron if you've got one – it'll help stop you getting too messy!

Go Green!

Hello Kitty loves pink, but she loves green too – especially when it means helping the environment. Follow Hello Kitty's top tips on how to be good to the environment and make the world a cleaner and more super place!

Bagged it!

Carry a fabric bag with you wherever you go, so that you don't have to use plastic bags when you go shopping! You can buy a cheap plain one, and customise it yourself using sequins, buttons and fabric paint – super-cute, and super green!

Beautiful Bottles

Instead of buying drinks in bottles every day, take your own bottle wherever you go. You can have it decorated however you want; either by getting one you like from a shop, or reusing one from home that you decorate yourself. Best of all, it means you can take whichever drinks you want to school – from fruit juice and squash to home-made smoothies.

Blown away!

You can save electricity (and the environment) by letting your hair dry naturally instead of using a hairdryer. And for a super-cool wavy look, try plaiting it in lots of little plaits before letting it dry, and then shaking them out. Gorgeous!

Bin-tastic!

You can recycle everywhere – even in your bedroom! Decorate two ordinary bins however you want so they match your bedroom; Hello Kitty likes hers to be sparkly! One can be for normal rubbish, and the other is for paper, plastic, and other things you can add to the family recycling each week. Super green!

Jammin' Jars

Wash out and reuse food jars and pots, decorate them, and use them to hold all your bits and pieces. Hair clips, coins, flowers and jewellery can look even prettier on display in your bedroom in a jar decorated with a pretty ribbon or some bright fabric.

Turn the page for a sneak peek at

Hello Kitty

and friends'

next adventure...

The Dance Camp

Hello Kitty fastened the pink bow in her
hair and then twirled in front of her bedroom
mirror. She was really excited! It was the first
day of holidays and she was about to go on a
week-long dance and music camp. Her three
best friends were going to be there too – Dear
Daniel, Fifi and Tammy. Together they made up

the Friendship Club. They had meetings where they baked and made things, had sleepovers and went on outings. They also liked to make up rules about friendship, things like Good Friends Make Hard Things Easy To Do.

Just then, Hello Kitty's bedroom door opened and her twin sister Mimmy looked in. Mimmy had a blue bow in her hair; she always wore her bow on the right and Hello Kitty always wore her bow on the left so that people could tell them apart. It was time to go to camp. They didn't want to be late on their first day!

Hello Kitty grabbed her bag and ran downstairs with Mimmy. Papa was holding the car keys and heading out the door as Mama came into the hall, carrying a couple of full rubbish bags.

What was she doing, asked Hello Kitty? Mama smiled and explained that she had decided to spend the day having a good sort out of their old toys – the ones they used to play with. Some were broken and needed to be thrown away, and others could be given to charity.

Mimmy looked a bit anxious. Mama wouldn't get rid any of the toys they still played with, would she?

Mama promised she wouldn't throw any toys away without checking with Mimmy and Hello Kitty first. All she was going to do that day was sort them out, and then when the girls came home they could decide which toys they would like to give away. It was such a shame to have toys in the house that they never played with, she said — it would be much better for them to be given to younger children who would really enjoy them…

Find out what happens next in...

Coming soon!

The Dance Camp
· A HELLO KITTY ADVENTURE ·

The Big Race

The Makeover Party
· A HELLO KITTY ADVENTURE ·

The Cupcake Mystery
· A HELLO KITTY ADVENTURE ·

The Award Adventure
· A HELLO KITTY ADVENTURE ·

The Halloween Parade
· A HELLO KITTY ADVENTURE ·

The Magazine Mix-Up

The TV Star
· A HELLO KITTY ADVENTURE ·

Collect all of the Hello Kitty and Friends Stories!

The Friendship Club

The School Trip

The Summer Fair

The Pop Princess

The Wedding Day

The Beach Holiday

The Treasure Hunt

The Talent Show

The Christmas Present
TWO SPECIAL CHRISTMAS STORIES

Christmas Special: • • • •
Two Stories in One!